For everyone everywhere

Cry whenever you need to.

Hendrix
the
Hedgehog

Hendrix the hedgehog and Myla the mouse,
Were neighbours and very best chums,

Both lived in a field, by a stream, near a bridge,
And they spent their days eating plums.

Now Myla was quiet, thoughtful and shy,
She listened much more than she spoke,

But Hendrix was booming, rambunctious and loud,
And loved nothing more than a joke.

Though different, they shared their love of all food,
Bananas and pumpkins and bread.

But one bright spring morning, disaster had struck,
Hendrix screamed as he rolled out of bed.

His pancake pillow and blanket of cheese
Had disappeared in the night.

Myla's stepping stone eggs and banana peel slide
Were now such a chaotic sight.

"My bike and my cars and my basketball too,
They're ruined!" Hendrix cried out.
Myla looked all around at the mess by her feet,
But she didn't scream or shout.

"Look right over here, a trail of crumbs!"
Myla calmly said as she strode.
The pair hurried off, eyes glued to the ground,
'Til they came to a fork in the road.

"I see footprints this way!" Hendrix bellowed aloud,
"Here's one! And another!" he cried.
A flash of grey dashed from a branch in a tree,
And the pair scuttled on, side by side.

"Stop!" Myla whispered,
"here's part of your chair."
Hendrix wailed, "it really can't be!"

A big chunky tear rolled down his small cheek
As he picked up a piece by a tree.

"Are you crying?" a voice spoke from somewhere up high,
"You really shouldn't do that."
Hendrix looked up, and saw a cat on the fence.
"Why not?" he frowned, as he sat.

"Someone might see you, it's really not good,"
The cat continued to speak.
But Hendrix still sobbed, his tears falling fast;
"Crying does not make me weak."

The mouse and the hedgehog plodded on once again,
Spotting some scraps near a slug.

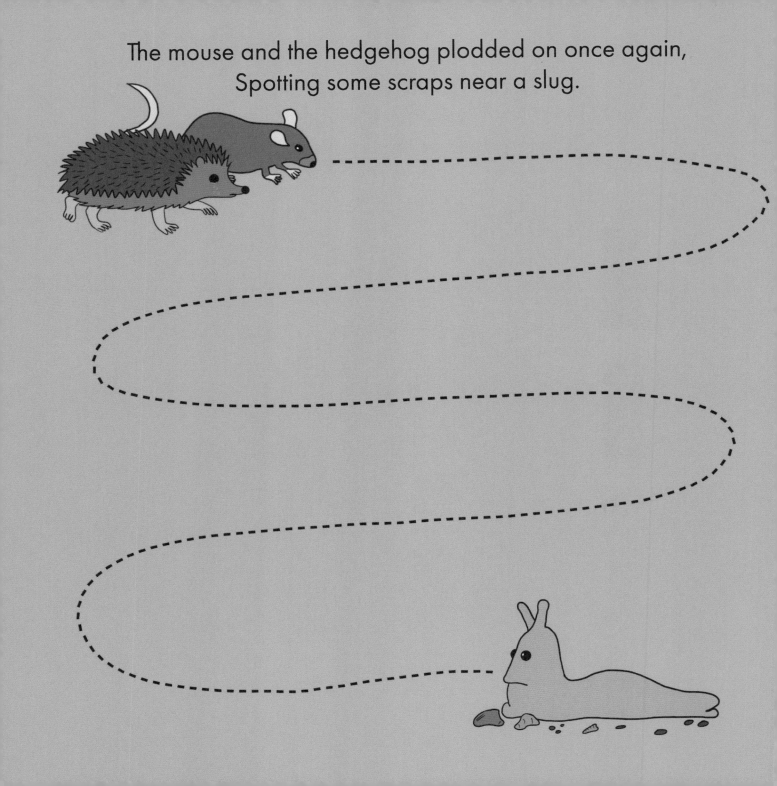

Hendrix kept crying, all his sad flowing out,
And Myla paused to give him a hug.

"Oh no! Are those tears?" the slug asked with a grimace,
"Hedgehogs are not meant to cry."
But Hendrix was bold and defiant and sure,
"When I'm sad I sob and I sigh."

Myla spoke softly, "I'm proud of you friend,
You should never be made to feel bad.
Crying and talking and sobbing and hugging,
Are the best things to do when you're sad."

A squeaking sound stopped the pair in their tracks,
Then a grunt and a giggle of glee!
Hendrix crept closer and put his ear to the air,
As two squirrels leapt down from a tree.

"Mason! Melissa!" a voice screeched from a branch,
  "Where did you find all this food?"
The beady-eyed squirrels froze in mid-air
  As they noticed this hedgehog's sad mood.

"Are those tears I see? I thought hedgehogs were tough,"
One squirrel said to the other.
"You must hide your sadness, can't dare let it out,"
The small squirrel agreed with her brother.

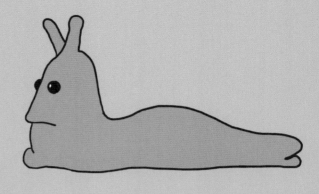

Hendrix was sad and confused and annoyed,
"Actually you've got it all wrong.
Whether I'm a hedgehog or a slug or a pig,
I can cry and I can sob all day long."

"Whenever I'm sad I might run, walk or roll,

Sometimes I just sing or I shout.

I might draw, I might chat, I might hug a close friend,
But I will let my feelings come out."

The squirrels looked shocked, and a little in awe,
"You don't think crying makes you odd?"
"If I need to, I weep, it's the best way to live,
You should try it," Hendrix said with a nod.

"Mason! Melissa!" the voice came again,
And now a mother squirrel appeared.
"What's this? And this?" she said holding some food,
Hendrix gasped; it was worse than he feared.

"My toys! My chair," he screamed after his shock.
"You've nibbled our things through and through."
"I'm sorry, we were hungry," the small squirrel squeaked,
"But we'll fix them for you, good as new."

The group scurried around finding leaves, twigs and mud,
To patch up the holes in the gear.
Hendrix was sad to see his belongings destroyed,
And he released another small tear.

Mother squirrel brought over a plate full of nuts,
And a croissant, some berries and cake.
"I'm sorry you're sad dear, but I'll sit here and listen.
You can tell me about your heart break."

Hendrix smiled softly, then spoke with a chuckle,
"I just needed my time to be sad.
Now I've cried and I've hugged and I've mended and talked,
Things don't seem nearly as bad."

The squirrels and Myla helped rebuild the things,
And Hendrix danced round full of glee!
"Thank you, they're perfect; better than before!"
And the friends settled down with some tea.

Now, it doesn't matter if you're a boy or a girl,
Or an uncle, a mum or a dad,
You can cry when you need to, you can scream, weep or sob,
Emotions are for all; they're not bad.

So remember the next time when you have a wobble,
And the tears are stinging your eyes,
Hug a friend, sit and chat, and just let the tears fall.
Showing your feelings is so wise.

Dear Parents,

I write this book from the deepest part of my heart, as a mum of four precious boys. I have only one request; please let your children, both boys and girls, cry. No, not let. Please *encourage* them to cry. Does this sound like madness to you? Let me explain.

I cringe when I hear people saying 'Boys don't cry', or 'Man up' or even 'Don't be a girl'. Boys and girls are very different, I am fully aware. But somehow, somewhere along the way we seem to have got a little confused. Emotions are a natural thing, we all feel them and need to express them. And yet we seem to be surrounded by a culture of 'boys-need-to-hold-it-all-in-and-be-brave-and-not-show-one-bit-of-emotion' type believers. Why do we do this? Why do we allow this to be said to our children, the next generation?

Hug them. Talk about their feelings. Notice their sadness. Encourage them to cry if they need to. Do art therapy with them. Help them to start a diary. These are not weird and wacky ideas for eccentric parenting. They should just be everyday life.

With heartfelt gratitude,

Naomi

Printed in Great Britain
by Amazon